ROSA
at the
ZOO

by Joy Cowley
illustrated by Clare Bowes

LEARNING
MEDIA®

Dad took us to the zoo.
"Let's go and see the monkeys," said Dad.
"Me, too!" said Rosa.

We lifted Rosa up.
"I like monkeys," said Rosa.
"Let's go and see the lions," I said.
"Me, too!" said Rosa.

3

We lifted Rosa up.
She looked at the lion.
It walked up and down,
up and down,
looking at us.

Then the lion roared.
Rosa cried.
"I don't like lions," she said.

We went to see the elephant.
It was having a bath.

Rosa likes baths.
She looked at the elephant
and said, "Me, too! Me, too!"

"No, Rosa," said Dad.
"That bath is for the elephant."

The elephant looked at Rosa.
It lifted up its trunk.
WOOOOOSH!
Rosa was wet all over.

"There you are," said Dad.
"No bath.
But you did get a shower."